CW00841474

THE ROUNDABOUT HORSE

**Story by
H. E. TODD**

**Pictures by
VAL BIRO**

Picture
Knight

Before Flanaghan's Fair opened in the High Street, Bobby Brewster was flattered to be shown round the fairground by the owner himself. Mr Flanaghan was proud of the grand motor-driven roundabout right in the middle of the fair, with cars and motor-cycles whizzing round as the music blared, and there were many exciting sideshows and stalls.

Tucked away between the stalls was a rather sad little roundabout worked by a man who turned a wheel to make animals and birds glide gently round and round and up and down and up and down.

'This is the first roundabout I ever owned,' said Mr Flanaghan. 'People don't seem to find it exciting any more, and I'm afraid it is beginning to look rather tatty.'

But there was one animal on that roundabout that caught Bobby's eye – a white horse covered with red spots and with proud flaring nostrils. Bobby even gave that horse a name – Snorter – and he thought that when the fair opened he simply must have a ride on Snorter even if it was not exciting.

And what a good thing he did, for it was the start of an amazing adventure.

Bobby fondly patted Snorter before mounting, and Snorter turned his head round and said, 'Please help me.' Bobby was so surprised at hearing a roundabout horse talk, or any horse for that matter, that all he could answer was, 'How?'

'I'm tired of chasing an ostrich with a silly expression on its face day after day,' explained Snorter. 'All we ever do is glide round and round and up and down and up and down all the time. That may be good enough for an ostrich, but I'm a horse, and horses can gallop and jump. I want to be a real horse for a change.'

Then the roundabout started, and as Bobby was riding him Snorter said, 'There are notices up all along the High Street about a Grand Horse Show in Mantles Green Meadow at 2.30 p.m. next Saturday. That is just a short way from here. If I can hide myself near the entrance before opening time, will you ride me in and enter me for some of the events?'

'Certainly,' said Bobby, feeling excited at the idea, 'but I've never ridden a real horse before.'

'Never mind,' said Snorter, 'I promise to behave myself.'

Sure enough, on Saturday afternoon, Snorter was waiting. Bobby mounted, held the reins tightly, and rode him into the ring where the horses were being shown. The spectators had never seen a white horse with red spots at a Horse Show before and they clapped so loudly that Bobby thought Snorter might win a prize.

The judge was Colonel Danvers, a gentleman with a red face and a bristly moustache. He patted all the horses on their flanks to see how silky they felt, and when he came to Snorter there was such a loud pat that he said, 'Goodness gracious me, this horse feels like wood.'

Then he took a penknife from his pocket and started to scrape, and when one of Snorter's red spots scraped off he cried, 'It *is* wood! I can't give a prize at a Horse Show to a wooden horse. Take him away!'

Bobby was disappointed, but then decided to enter Snorter for the next event, which was a race. As the horses stood at the starting line the people saw Snorter's proud flaring nostrils and said to each other, 'There's the winner'.'

But he wasn't. Colonel Danvers shouted, 'Go', and all Snorter could do was run round and round in circles because that is what he had been doing all his life on a roundabout. He bumped into other horses and then they crashed into each other, and some of the riders fell off and there was pandemonium.

Colonel Danvers was so angry that he turned even redder and his moustache bristled even more.

'Remove that wooden horse from the field,' he demanded. 'He has no right to be at a Horse Show at all!'

Bobby rode Snorter away feeling rather ashamed, but he needn't have done.

'I'm fed up with this,' said Snorter. 'Even if I *am* a wooden horse that runs round and round in circles I'm jolly well going to prove that I can jump.'

And to the amazement of the crowd, with Bobby cling-
ing desperately round his neck, Snorter charged towards
the hedge and soared right over it into Tomkins' Meadow.

Mr Flanaghan himself happened to be standing there just as Snorter landed.

'Where did he come from?' he cried.

'He jumped,', said Bobby, when he had recovered his breath.

'What – right over that hedge?' asked Mr Flanaghan.

'Yes,' said Bobby proudly, 'and it's two metres high.'

'Goodness gracious me,' said Mr Flanaghan, and then he turned to Snorter.

'Well, up till now you may only have been a wooden horse gliding round and round after a silly looking ostrich, but if you can jump like that you're wasted on an ordinary old roundabout. I'm going to scrap all those other animals and birds and I'm going to have you painted up and put on the roundabout all by yourself with a lot of fences to jump over, and charge fifty pence a time for such an exciting ride.'

So that is what happened – and now everyone is happy.
Mr Flanaghan, because people queue up to pay fifty pence
a time for a roundabout ride all by themselves. The people
who pay the fifty pences, because the thrilling ride is well
worth it. Bobby Brewster, because every now and then Mr
Flanaghan allows him to have a free ride. But, best of all,
dear old Snorter himself, who can not only jump to his
heart's content, but is very proud to be on a special round
-about all by himself with a large notice by the side
announcing:

★ SNORTER ★
The Wonderful Jumping
ROUNDABOUT HORSE

British Library Cataloguing in Publication Data

Todd, H. E.
  The roundabout horse.
  Rn: Balint Stephan Biro   I. Title
  823´.914[J]   PZ7
  ISBN 0-340-42392-7

Text copyright © H. E. Todd 1978
Illustrations copyright © Val Biro 1978

All rights reserved

First published 1978 by Hodder and Stoughton Children's Books
This edition first published 1988 by Picture Knight

Published by Hodder and Stoughton Paperbacks,
a division of Hodder and Stoughton Ltd,
Mill Road, Dunton Green, Sevenoaks, Kent TN13 2YE

Editorial office: 47 Bedford Square, London WC1B 3DP

Printed in Great Britain by Springbourne Press Limited,
Basildon, Essex